THE CREATION OF MONITOR

Written by Neil Morris

Illustrated by Simon Howden

Scholastic Publications Ltd.,
10 Earlham Street, London WC2H 9RX, UK
First published in the UK by Scholastic Publications Limited, 1988
Copyright © 1987 King Features Entertainment, Inc./King Features Syndicate, Inc.
Distribution by Yaffa Character Licensing, London
DEFENDERS OF THE EARTH and associated characters are trademarks owned
by and used under licence from King Features Syndicate Inc.

ISBN 0 590 70920 8

Made and printed in Hong Kong
Typeset in Times Roman by AKM Associates (UK) Ltd,
Ajmal House, Hayes Road, Southall, London

Hippo Books
Scholastic Publications Ltd
London

A howling wind whipped across the barren
landscape of the arctic wastes. Two ice robots
fought their way through the blizzard. Stopping
their snowmobile at the edge of a chasm, the
robots turned on their squirter. A controlled
stream of water arched across the chasm,
quickly freezing to form a soaring bridge of ice.
The snowmobile rolled across the bridge.
Ming the Merciless sat in his throne room,
watching his ice robots on Octon's viewscreen.

"The work on Ice Station Earth is going well, O Mighty Emperor," said Octon, Ming's computer servant.

"But much too slowly!" snapped Ming. "My plans to conquer planet Earth cannot proceed until my base is completed. Order all activities accelerated!"

Before Octon could obey, a warning klaxon sounded. Ming's eyes narrowed as he looked at Octon. "What is this interruption?" he asked

5

impatiently.

The scene on Octon's viewscreen changed to a group of sleek spaceships. "A fleet of alien ships approaching Earth, Sire," reported Octon.

"I do not recognize them," Ming told the eight-legged robot. "Break into their code and find out who they are." Octon's computer lights flashed as he worked hard to break the code.

"Sire," Octon said at last. "I'm picking up transmissions from a computer using Flash Gordon's code."

Ming stood up at once, his fists clenched at his sides. "Flash Gordon?" he cried. "Determine the source of the transmissions. If it *is* Gordon, I will destroy the earthman once and for all!"

. . . . . .

Flash Gordon was unaware that the evil Ming was tracking him. He was busy at Mandrake the Magician's mansion, working with his son, Rick, on a brilliant new computer. "It won't be long now," said Rick, sitting at one of the computer's control stations.

"You've been saying that for the last two hours!" laughed L.J.

Mandrake was quick to defend young Rick. "A few hours is not long to wait for the creation of Dynak-X," he said, "the most advanced computer ever seen on Earth!" Mandrake twirled a globe of the Earth on his finger. He threw it towards L.J., but as he went to catch it, it vanished!

"Dynak-X will be the first computer to have a human essence at its centre," Flash told the others.

"I don't understand," Jedda whispered to her father.

"We have the crystal from Ming's evil Inquisitor machine," the Phantom replied. "It contains the essence of Rick's mother."

Rick held the crystal close. Then he placed it carefully in a special slot on the computer. The crystal gently slid into place.

"She's ready, Dad," Rick told Flash.

"Dynak-X is your creation, son," Flash replied. "*You* activate her."

Rick needed no second invitation. He pressed a red button, and the computer's screen started crackling. "Maybe Dynak-X can help us find a place for our new headquarters," Kshin said to Zuffy, his little friend. Rick adjusted some of the computer's controls, and suddenly the screen cleared to show a pretty face.

"Attention all personnel," said Dynak-X's voice. "Unidentified ships approaching Central City."

"Unidentified, but not unfriendly, I hope!" said Mandrake anxiously.

"If they're friends of Ming's, we're in big trouble!" said L.J.

"No trouble!" yelled Flash. "Those are Krel ships, and they're old friends of mine. They are here to help us build our new headquarters." As he spoke, Dynak-X's screen changed again and showed the strange figure of an alien being.

"Welcome to Earth, Morcon!" Flash said warmly.

"We are always glad to help an old friend, Flash," the alien replied. "Tell me, have you chosen a name yet for your new base?"

"We've decided to call it Monitor," Flash replied proudly.

"From which we will *monitor* the activities of the tyrant, Ming," Mandrake added.

The Defenders of the Earth could not know that at that very moment Ming the Merciless was

tracking them through their own transmissions. They watched the Krel fleet on Dynak-X's viewscreen. Suddenly laser blasts appeared as if from nowhere, hitting two Krel ships. "Ming's roboships!" yelled Lothar. "They must have followed the Krel ships to our location."

"They've broken Dynak's code," said Flash. "She needs more shielding!"

Morcon's strange face appeared on the screen. "Flash!" he shouted. "We're in trouble!"

"Just hang on, Morcon," Flash replied. "I'm coming up!" He knew that words were no longer enough. The situation required action. Flash ran to the large garage next to Mandrake's mansion, opened the doors, and blasted off at once in his spaceship.

Mandrake ran outside and saw that Ming's robofighters were approaching fast. "We're sitting ducks here," he thought, "unless . . ." He decided on an illusion. As the robofighters closed in, Mandrake made the mansion appear to rise in the air! Ming's robots were mystified.

They swerved to avoid the mansion, and two
robofighters crashed into each other. Mandrake
doffed his top hat and laughed. "Mandrake's
mansion-moving company, at your service!" he
joked.

Back inside, Lothar and Dynak-X were
guiding Flash towards the other robofighters.
Kshin was getting very excited. "Come on, blast
'em, Flash!" he cried. "Show them what the
Defenders can do!"

Mandrake frowned. "Please, Kshin," he said.
"We're trying to concentrate. Go and find a

place where you can stay out of trouble." Kshin
was annoyed. He grabbed Zuffy, marched out of
the room, and slammed the door.

"Kshin!" Mandrake called after him. But
there was no reply.

"Don't worry, my friend," said Lothar. "He'll
be okay. I sometimes think it's easier to deal
with Ming than to understand young people!"

. . . . . .

16

Kshin and Zuffy climbed the rocks outside
Mandrake's mansion. They heard loud
explosions and laser blasts, and looked up to see
the aerial battle between Flash and his Krel
friends on the one side and Ming's robofighters
on the other. "Get 'em, Flash!" Kshin cried, as
his hero zapped two robofighters at once. In his

excitement Kshin picked up a rock and hurled it at a robofighter as it zoomed past. The rock hit the enemy craft, and it exploded! Kshin couldn't believe it. He and Zuffy just looked at each other. "Wow!" said Kshin at last.

Pieces of hot metal rained down on them from the crashed robofighter. "We'd better get out of here," Kshin told little Zuffy, picking him up. But just then a laser blast cut them off. They were trapped! All they could do was watch the battle going on overhead.

Ming's robofighters were still giving Flash Gordon a hard time. Then, as Kshin watched, the Krel ships formed up into the shape of an enormous cone. Flash's ship suddenly soared into view and flew around the Krel fleet to the back of the cone. The robofighters swooped, when suddenly all the ships of the Krel fleet fired at once. The robofighters were engulfed in a solid cylinder of white energy. They didn't stand a chance.

Kshin could certainly see that Flash and Morcon had worked together before. He and Zuffy jumped up in triumph, but just then Kshin saw another ship approaching. "Watch out, Zuffy!" he cried. "They missed one of the robofighters!"

The lone ship zoomed towards them, piloted by Garax, head of the robot fleet. He reported

to Ming, who was watching the action on the
screen in his throne room. When Ming saw
Kshin and Zuffy, he turned to his computer
servant. "Octon," he said, "confirm the origin of
that creature with the Earth boy."

"Yes, Sire," replied Octon. "The creature is a
Zuffoid from Mongo."

Ming was triumphant. "I knew it!" he cried.
"And that boy was with Gordon. Garax, I want
the boy and the Zuffoid captured . . . alive!"

Garax was surprised. "Alive, mighty Ming?"
he asked.

Ming's eyes glowed red. "Yes," he replied. "With the boy as my hostage, Gordon will walk into my hands and I'll crush the so-called Defenders of the Earth!"

Garax knew better than to disobey his master.
   As his roboship flew towards Kshin, two ice
robots jumped from a hatch. Anti-gravity beams
from their belts helped them to float gently
down to the rocks. Kshin saw the ice robots
heading straight for them. "We've got to hide,
Zuffy!" he shouted. They both ducked behind a
huge boulder.
   When they landed, the ice robots immediately
opened fire with their laser weapons. They

blasted the boulder away, revealing a huge tunnel behind it. Kshin and Zuffy ran into the tunnel, and were astonished to find inside a huge cavern full of stalactites, stalagmites and a pearly glow.

"Imagine!" said Kshin. "Right next door to Mandrake's place, and we never even knew it was here!" But there was no time to enjoy the view. The ice robots were marching after them.

"Run for it!" shouted Kshin. They could hear the robots' footsteps echoing off the walls. Then suddenly they came to a sheer drop. There was nothing they could do. As the robots grabbed at

them, the ground gave way, and Kshin and Zuffy fell.

But they were lucky — it was not a big drop. When they hit the bottom, they sat up and looked around. They found that they had fallen on to a strip of rock next to a hissing, bubbling river of molten lava. Behind them was a wall of rock. Then they heard the footsteps again. The ice robots were on the far side of the lava, and they were starting to wade in! But that was their big mistake. The lava was much too hot for them, and they instantly began to melt and sink. They were still firing their laser beams as they disappeared beneath the molten lava.

The laser fire smashed a hole in the rock behind Kshin. "Let's hope this tunnel will lead us out of here," he said to Zuffy, as they stepped through the hole. On the other side it was pitch dark. They couldn't see a thing. "Sure is dark in here, Zuffy," said Kshin. "Stay close, okay?"

Just then they heard a loud growling noise. "What was *that?*" cried Kshin, scared out of his wits. Zuffy squealed and chattered, as frightened as his master. Then suddenly the whole place was bathed in light, and a voice said, "Kisa was right. There *is* somebody in Mandrake's wine cellar!" Kshin and Zuffy held each other tight, both blinking against the sudden bright light.

"How can you two see with the lights off?" asked the voice. It was Jedda — with Kisa, her pet panther! And they *were* in Mandrake's wine cellar! Kshin and Zuffy looked at each other, amazed and relieved.

. . . . . .

When Kshin told the others what had happened, they asked Dynak-X to investigate the mountain next to Mandrake's mansion. The computer's screen showed an X-ray view of the mountain, with tunnels and caverns. Dynak-X spoke: "According to the data I am receiving, the mountain includes a cavern large enough for a small city."

"Which is perfect," said Flash, "because that's exactly what it's going to be. I don't think we'll ever find a better place for Monitor headquarters than the one Kshin and Zuffy discovered."

Kshin was delighted, and slapped Zuffy's palm. "Kshin has the makings of a real Defender," said Mandrake, "if only he can learn to follow orders!" Kshin blushed. He knew that Mandrake was right.

Dynak-X went on with her report. "There is one piece of data which may alter the plan to locate Monitor inside this mountain." The

Defenders exchanged puzzled glances. "The mountain is a volcano," Dynak-X went on, "and it is not entirely extinct." Dynak-X's screen was filled with streams of lava.

"Even we Krel would have difficulty building a structure to withstand a volcanic eruption," said Morcon.

But Jedda had an idea. "We could cap the active shaft of the volcano, and harness the

26

geothermal energy for power," she said thoughtfully.

Rick Gordon laughed. "Trust Jedda to think of a simple solution to our energy problem!" he said.

"Jedda is correct," the Phantom said firmly. "Her idea will give us an endless supply of energy."

"Right! Well, let's get going!" said Flash, never one to waste time.

Morcon and the Krel were expert engineers, and set to work at once. Laser cutters sliced through walls of tunnels, leaving flat surfaces. They melted the excess rock, and sucked it away in big hoses. Krel cranes lifted huge beams into place, and welded them tight in a shower of sparks. They built bridges, buttresses and hallways. And in the centre of all this was the crown, built in the great central cavern on a pneumatic lift.

Morcon supervised the building work from the control centre on the cavern wall. His Krel builders worked at super speed, and their machines did in hours what would otherwise have taken weeks. Morcon explained to the Phantom and Jedda: "Once the crown is finished, it will rise on the shafts through an opening in the crater. That will be the final stage of construction."

"Something is bothering you, Jedda," the

Phantom said when they were alone. "Are you not happy in our new home?"

"I have no desire to live here, father," Jedda replied. "Our home is with the jungle beasts of Africa."

"But we must stay with the others," her father
said, "to help defend the Earth. I can't allow
you to return to Africa alone. I am only
concerned for your welfare."

Jedda put her arms round her father. "I
know," she said. The Phantom could only hope
that one day his daughter would get used to life
at Monitor. Through the control centre
windows, he saw a line of Krel ships rolling
through a huge opening in the mountain.

"It was a good idea to store our ships inside
the mountain," Flash Gordon said to Morcon.
"It's much safer. If Ming attacks, our ships
won't be so vulnerable."

In his throat room, Ming was furious that his
attack on Flash had gone so wrong. When
Garax returned, his master rounded on him.
"Garax, you fool!" he snarled. "Not only have
you lost a fleet of robofighters, and a phalanx of
ice robots, but you have lost the boy as well!"

Octon came to Garax's aid. "Sire, I detect
massive amounts of power being used in almost
the same location," he said. "But *inside* the
mountain."

"It must be the Defenders' base!" cried Ming.

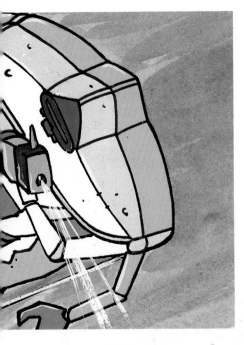

"O Mighty Ming," Garax pleaded. "Let me send a small party of ice robots into their base, and destroy it from within."

Ming's eyes narrowed. "Very well, Garax," he snapped. "You may do so. But this time I will not tolerate failure!"

Garax chose his two strongest ice robots for the task. He flew them to the volcano, where his roboship dropped them. Using their anti-gravity beams, they floated through an opening in the mountainside and into Monitor.

When they saw Flash Gordon talking to Morcon, they swooped at them and fired their laser guns. Flash and Morcon quickly dived for cover.

The ice robots fired in all directions. Laser beams flew everywhere, setting off a landslide that covered the opening of the cavern with rock.

"Our ships are trapped inside!" yelled Flash. "If Ming attacks now, we're helpless! We've got to stop those ice robots before they destroy Monitor!" He ran towards the control centre. The ice robots were floating about the cavern in mid-air, but he was too fast for them.

As soon as he was in the control centre, Flash pushed the operating levers. "A Krel machine that can cut rock can also cut those ice robots down to size!" he muttered. The laser rock-cutter swivelled like a cannon turret and fired short laser bursts. But the robots moved too fast even for this.

Watching from below, the Phantom could see that superhuman strength was needed. He raised his fists above his head. "By jungle law, the

33

ghost who walks calls forth the power of ten tigers!" he cried. At once he was surrounded by a force field. He ran up the arm of a crane and leapt over to a cable suspended from the cavern roof. He swung from one cable to the next towards the ice robots.

"Good work, Phantom!" shouted Flash. "Keep going and lead them into my range!"

The robots fired at the Phantom, but he was

forcing them closer to Flash. When the robots were in the right position, Flash pressed the start button of a huge cement squirter. A stream of liquid cement hit the ice robots. Both plummeted down, stiffening as they fell. They hit the ground with a tremendous crash and shattered into thousands of pieces.

"Tut-tut, what a mess," said Mandrake, smiling to himself. He pointed, and magically lifted the broken pieces into a skip.

"You're a handy man to have around, Mandrake," said Lothar with a laugh.

Once again Garax was called before his master.
"Your robots follow your example with great
fidelity, Garax!" yelled Ming. "They are totally
incompetent! Octon, I want the Defenders' base
to end up like Garax's worthless robots. Let this
be a foretaste of what I have in store for all who
oppose me!"

Ming ordered Octon to despatch another fleet
of robofighters to the volcano, and at once.

Inside Monitor, Dynak-X quickly picked up
the approaching roboships and sent out a
warning. Flash was worried that, with the

mountain sealed off, they had no way to defend themselves. But Lothar had an idea. "Dynak," he said, "I want you to transmit an SOS signal from the top of the volcano."

"But that would be nothing more than a homing signal for Ming," said Morcon.

"Exactly!" cried Lothar.

Dynak-X did as requested, and Garax soon picked up the SOS as he and his robofighters approached the volcano. "We will respond to the distress signal by putting them out of their misery!" he snarled, and ordered all his ships to target their laser beams on the mountaintop.

They all blasted at once, and blew the top right off the mountain!

"They fell for it!" shouted Flash, watching on Dynak's screen and feeling the whole base shake violently. "They've opened the crater for us!"

"Perfect!" said Lothar. "Now we can raise the crown and take off!"

This was the moment Rick Gordon had been waiting for. He watched on Dynak-X's screen as the crown rose up on its shafts. When it reached the top of the mountain, Rick pressed a button to flood the space round the crown with water, forming a lake. Soon the launch bay doors were clear of water and rock. This was Flash's cue. He rushed off with Rick and L.J. to attack the enemy robofighters.

They took off from the new launch bay, and aimed their lasers at the robofighters. One of Ming's stricken ships crashed on the volcano, and a crack formed in the geothermal cap at the base of Monitor's shafts. At once the alarm sounded inside the base. Dynak-X flashed red emergency lights. "Warning!" said the computer's voice. "We are losing geothermal pressure!"

Morcon was sitting at Dynak-X's control panel. He watched the screen carefully, trying to find the pressure point in the geosystem. Then Dynak-X flashed a red blip at the end of a long narrow tunnel. "According to my calculations," said the computer, "an explosion at this precise point would relieve pressure on the system." Lothar took a small grenade from his belt. "This megabomb has enough blasting power to do the

trick," he said.

The Phantom held out his hand. "I'll plant the device," he said.

"No, none of us can do it," said Morcon. "The location is at the end of a long, slanting shaft barely big enough for a child."

"Or a cat . . ." Jedda said quietly, kneeling down and putting her hand on Kisa's head. The black panther purred as Jedda told her what she had to do, and placed the grenade gently in her mouth. Then Jedda put her hands to her temples, concentrated hard, and used her telekinetic powers to guide Kisa to the precise spot in the geosystem.

Kisa crept through the narrow tunnels and, when Jedda told her to, put the explosive down gently. "Now come, Kisa! Come, fast!" cried Jedda. The panther ran back through the tunnel, and got back to her mistress just as the explosion tore through the whole system. She had done her job well.

Lothar took over the computer operations with Dynak-X, and immediately submerged Monitor's crown beneath the surface of the artificial lake. He then released debris to the surface of the lake to make Ming think that they had been wiped out by the explosion.

Morcon had already examined the explosion damage, and he took the Phantom and Jedda to see what he had found. It was a new cavern.

"The natural steam escaping from the active part of the volcano keeps it humid and at a constant 27 degrees Celsius," Morcon told them.

"Father!" cried Jedda. "It's just like the climate of our home in Africa!"

The Phantom was pleased. "It will be the perfect location for a second Skull Cave," he said. He and Jedda hugged each other, and Morcon laughed happily. The new Monitor base offered even more than the Defenders had hoped for.

. . . . . .

The plan to fool Ming had worked. Watching the explosion at Monitor on his screen, he laughed like a demon. "A volcanic eruption!" he bellowed. "The Defenders' base is destroyed! I have won!"

But just as he sat back on his throne, he saw a fleet of ships leaving the volcano. "Ah, the Krel ships are retreating," he gloated.

"With an escort from Flash Gordon, Sire!" said Octon, recognizing Flash's craft at the rear of the fleet. He seemed almost to enjoy Ming's misery. "The Defenders of the Earth are still alive, Sire!" his robotic voice chanted.

"But not for long!" cried Ming without conviction, as he slumped back on his throne and Flash's spacecraft filled his viewscreen.

THE DEFENDERS

THE PHANTOM
With strange supernatural powers taught by the natives of the Deep Woods, he draws on the strength of jungle animals and is the ultimate enemy of evil.

FLASH GORDON
The swashbuckling, square-jawed space pilot. He's fearless, resourceful, clever and strong – an intergalactic hero.

MANDRAKE THE MAGICIAN
Suave and sophisticated, moving only in the best of circles, he is adept at hypnotic deception. The master of illusion.

LOTHAR
The big, muscular but soft-spoken Jamaican is Mandrake's lifetime friend and protector. Easy-going and charming, but with fists of steel!